PUFFIN BOOKS

TEN IN A BED

Allan Ahlberg trained as a teacher at Sunderland College of Education. After a series of jobs including postman, grave-digger, soldier and plumber's mate, he spent ten years teaching. He lives just outside Leicester together with his wife, Janet, and their daughter, Jessica. Allan Ahlberg has created many books for children, and has worked previously with André Amstutz on the HAPPY FAMILIES series.

André Amstutz was born in Brighton. He studied art and design at Brighton School of Art and then joined an animation film company. He later began a career in advertising, becoming Art Director at an advertising agency. Since 1960 he has worked freelance, designing posters and illustrations for a wide variety of clients, and more recently has moved into publishing primarily as an illustrator of children's books.

Verse and Song

PLEASE MRS BUTLER
THE MIGHTY SLIDE
HEARD IT IN THE PLAYGROUND
THE MRS BUTLER SONGBOOK

Novels and Stories

WOOF!

Miscellaneous

The HAPPY FAMILIES *series*

With Janet Ahlberg

Picture Books

EACH PEACH PEAR PLUM
IT WAS A DARK AND STORMY NIGHT
PEEPO!
THE BABY'S CATALOGUE
THE CINDERELLA SHOW
STARTING SCHOOL

Novels and Stories

SON OF A GUN
THE BEAR NOBODY WANTED
JEREMIAH IN THE DARK WOODS
THE VANISHMENT OF THOMAS TULL
THE CLOTHES HORSE

Miscellaneous

THE OLD JOKE BOOK
THE HA HA BONK BOOK

Allan Ahlberg

Ten in a Bed

Illustrated by André Amstutz

PUFFIN BOOKS

PUFFIN BOOKS

Published by the Penguin Group
Penguin Books Ltd, 80 Strand, London WC2R 0RL, England
Penguin Putnam Inc., 375 Hudson Street, New York, New York 10014, USA
Penguin Books Australia Ltd, 250 Camberwell Road, Camberwell, Victoria 3124, Australia
Penguin Books Canada Ltd, 10 Alcorn Avenue, Toronto, Ontario, Canada M4V 3B2
Penguin Books India (P) Ltd, 11 Community Centre, Panchsheel Park, New Delhi – 110 017, India
Penguin Books (NZ) Ltd, Cnr Rosedale and Airborne Roads, Albany, Auckland, New Zealand
Penguin Books (South Africa) (Pty) Ltd, 24 Sturdee Avenue, Rosebank 2196, South Africa

Penguin Books Ltd, Registered Offices: 80 Strand, London WC2R 0RL England

www.penguin.com

First published by Granada Publishing 1983
Published by Viking Kestral 1989
Published in Puffin Books 1990
This edition has been produced exclusively for Nestlé Cheerios and
Honey Nut Cheerios 2003
1

Filmset in Sabon Linotron 202

Made and printed in England by Clays Ltd, St Ives plc

British Library Cataloguing in Publication Data
A CIP catalogue record for this book is available from the British Library

ISBN 0-141-31675-6

Contents

Too Many Bears 7

Esmerelda 17

The Clockwork Mouse 28

The Accident Book 40

Wilfred 49

Captain Dynamite Simon 61

A Kiss 71

Little Girl Sandwich 83

1

Too Many Bears

One evening a little girl named Dinah Price kissed her mum and dad goodnight, climbed the stairs, went into her room – and found three bears in her bed. These bears were a father bear, a mother bear and a baby bear. They were lying side by side, with the baby bear in the middle. They appeared to be sleeping.

Dinah Price knew a bit about bears. When she was an even littler girl, her mum used to tell her a story about some bears and the trouble they had had with another little girl named Goldilocks. So Dinah went up to the bed with the bears in it and said, 'Who's this sleeping in *my* bed?'

Straight away the bears opened their eyes and shouted, 'Us!' And they laughed – all three of them. They were only pretending to be asleep.

Dinah Price stood at the foot of the bed and looked at the bears. The evening sunlight was shining into the room. Through the open window came the sound of a lawn-mower. The next-door neighbour was cutting his grass.

The bears lay in the bed and looked at Dinah Price. From time to time they gave each other a little nudge and smiled. They did not seem embarrassed to be in someone else's bed. They showed no sign of leaving.

'What are you doing here?' said Dinah.

'Resting,' said the father bear.

'But how did you get in?'

'That would be telling. Maybe we climbed up the drainpipe.'

'Or down the chimney,' said the mother bear.

'Like Santa Claus!' the baby bear said.

'There isn't a chimney,' said Dinah. 'We've got central heating.'

At that moment through the open window came the chimes of an ice-cream van. The baby bear's little eyes lit up. 'Can we go home now?'

'No,' said the mother bear. 'We've only just got here.' Then, in a whisper to Dinah, she added, 'Take no notice. What he really wants is an ice-cream.'

'What are you whispering about?' said the baby bear. And he said, 'Can I have an ice-cream?'

'Wait and see,' said the mother bear.

Dinah Price thought for a minute. She would not have minded an ice-cream herself. She said, 'But shouldn't you be going home anyway? It's bedtime!'

'That's no problem,' said father bear. 'We're in bed.'

'Yes, but it's not yours – it's mine. And I have to go to sleep. I will get into trouble if I don't.'

'That's too bad,' said father bear. 'We like it here.'

'It's comfy,' the mother bear said.

The baby bear knelt up in the bed and whispered in his mother's ear. For the first time Dinah noticed he had her woolly duck in the bed with him. He must have taken it from the toy-box.

The mother bear nodded and smiled. Then the baby bear turned to Dinah. 'My mum says you could tell us a story!'

'A story?' Dinah frowned. 'You want *me* to tell *you* a story?'

'That's the idea,' said the mother bear.

Dinah Price thought for a minute. 'If I did tell you a story, would you promise to go home then – to your own beds?'

For a moment there was silence. The bears looked at each other. The baby bear whispered in his mother's ear again, and then his father's. After that all three of them spoke at once:

'Yes!'

'That's fair enough!'

'It's a promise!'

So Dinah Price pulled up her stool, picked up a book from her bedside table and began to read. Well, the truth is, she pretended to read, for she was making the story up. 'Once upon a time there were three bears –'

'Heard it already!' said the baby bear.

'No, you haven't,' said Dinah. 'This is a different one. Listen!'

And this is the story she told.

'Once upon a time there were three bears who lived together in a house of their own in a wood. One of them was a little, small, wee bear –'

'That's me!' the baby bear said.

'One was a middle-sized bear, and the other was a great, huge bear. One day these bears were out walking. They came to a neat little house on the edge of the wood. It had a red roof, yellow curtains and roses round the door. It was a girl named Goldilocks's house.'

'She's a little madam, that one,' the mother bear said.

'Well, the bears came up to the house and peeped through the window. Goldilocks was out. She had gone to play and have tea at her friend's house. So the bears opened the door and went in. They went down the hall and into the kitchen. There on the table was a delicious bowl of, er ... pineapple jelly, which Goldilocks was saving for her tea.'

'You said she was having tea at her friend's house,' the father bear said.

'Well, supper then. Anyway, there was the jelly. So first the great huge bear tasted it, but it was too sweet for him. Then the middle-sized bear tasted it, but it was too . . . wobbly.'

'I like it wobbly,' said the mother bear.

'Then the little, small, wee bear tasted the jelly and for him it was neither too sweet nor too wobbly, but just right. So he ate it *all* up.'

'Lovely!' The baby bear clapped his little paws. 'I want a drink of water.'

'No, you don't,' said the father bear. 'You have just had all that jelly.'

'And never even gave your poor old mother a lick of the spoon,' the mother bear said.

'Next the bears went upstairs to Goldilocks's bedroom. By this time all three of them were feeling tired from their walk; also, they were quite cheeky bears, as you can see. So they got into the bed and went to sleep. Then – this is the exciting part – then, Goldilocks came back!'

'From her friend's house,' the father bear said.

'That's it. Well, when Goldilocks saw the front door open, she said, "Wow – somebody has been at my front door and left it open." When she saw the empty bowl on the kitchen table, she said, "Wow – somebody has been at my pineapple jelly and eaten it all up."'

'Ha, ha!' said the baby bear.

'When she went upstairs and saw the bears in her bed, she said, "Wow – somebody has been sleeping in my bed – and they're still in it!"'

'Serves her right,' the father bear said.

And the baby bear said, 'Then what did she do?'

'She thought for a minute,' said Dinah, who was herself thinking for a minute. 'She thought for a minute and said, "Who's this sleeping in *my* bed?" And the bears woke up then, and they said, "Us!"'

'Weren't they only pretending to be asleep?' said the baby bear.

'No, they were really asleep. So then Goldilocks gave the three bears a good talking-to. She said they had no business being in her house, eating her pineapple jelly and sleeping in her bed.'

'She's got a nerve,' said the mother bear.

'Then the bears promised to leave if only Goldilocks would tell them a story; so she did. She told them a story and they listened and said thank-you-very-much. After that they went home – because a promise is a promise – they went home and –'

'Wait a minute,' the baby bear said. 'What was the story *she* told?'

'I don't remember. Anyway, that's another story!'

'I bet I know what it was,' said the mother bear. She began to smile. 'I bet it was like this: Goldilocks said, "Once upon a time there were three bears." Then the little, small, wee bear said he had heard it already –'

'I have heard it already *already*!' said the baby bear.

And the father bear said, 'My head is spinning. How many bears have we got now?'

'"Then the three bears went out for a walk,"' said the mother bear, '"and came to Goldilocks's house and went inside and ate her pineapple jelly."'

'Only the little, small, wee bear ate the jelly,' said the baby bear.

'No – they all ate it this time,' said the mother bear.

'In fact, come to think of it, the middle-sized bear ate most of it. Well, they ate the jelly and went upstairs for a lie-down, and Goldilocks came back and found them there and –'

'Told them to clear off out of it!' said Dinah, who was getting impatient.

'No, she didn't,' said the baby bear.

'Yes, she did. She said, "You bears get out of here or I will fetch my daddy, who is a hunter."'

'A hunter?' The baby bear looked puzzled. 'What's a hunter?'

'Don't answer that,' whispered the mother bear. 'We haven't told him about the hunters yet. He's too young.'

'What are you whispering about?' said the baby bear. And he said, 'What's a hunter?'

'A man,' the mother said. 'A man who cuts the trees down.'

'That's a wood-cutter!'

The mother bear turned to Dinah. 'Go on with the story.'

'Right,' said Dinah. 'So anyway, Goldilocks told the three bears about her daddy and his gun, and that was enough for them.'

'What's a gun?' said the baby bear.

'Don't answer *that*,' the mother bear said.

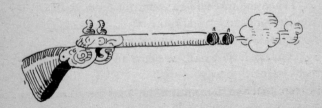

'That was enough for them,' said Dinah. 'They wasted no time, but jumped out of the bed, out of the window and ran off through the woods to their own house, their own pineapple jelly – and *their own beds*! The End.'

At this point Dinah slammed the book shut, startling the father bear, who had been dozing off. The mother bear sat up in the bed. 'That wasn't a bad story.' She yawned and stretched. 'Except for the last bit.'

Dinah Price stood up and put the book on her bedside table. It was darker in the room now. A smell of cut grass was coming through the open window. The noise of the mower had stopped. In a tree outside the window, birds were twittering. Downstairs the phone began to ring.

'Was Goldilocks's father really a "you-know-what"?' the mother bear said.

'What's a you-know-what?' said the baby bear.

'Yes, he was.' Dinah could feel her feet getting cold inside her slippers. 'He was a terror.' And she said, 'Are you going home now?'

'Certainly,' said the mother bear.

And the father bear said, 'We can take a hint.'

The three bears clambered out of the bed. The father bear and the mother bear tidied the bedclothes and plumped up the pillow.

'Do you have far to go?' said Dinah.

'That would be telling,' said the mother bear. 'It could be miles and miles!'

'Or just down the road,' the father bear said.

Then Dinah spotted the baby bear. He was trying to sneak off with her woolly duck. Luckily, the mother bear spotted him too. She made him give it back.

After that the three bears climbed out on to the window ledge, said goodbye to Dinah Price, went down the drainpipe and across the grass, waved goodbye to Dinah – who was watching them go – and disappeared into the rhododendron bushes at the far end of the garden.

The last words Dinah heard was the baby bear halfway down the drainpipe saying, 'Can we have pineapple jelly when we get home?' And his mother's reply: 'Wait and see.'

Dinah Price shut the window and pulled the curtains across. She said to herself, 'I will tell my friend about this tomorrow.' After that she got into the bed – still warm from the bears – and slept till morning.

2

Esmerelda

The next day Dinah Price got up, got dressed and had her breakfast. She had cornflakes with the top of the milk on them, a piece of her dad's toast and marmalade, a cup of tea and an orange. She told her dad about the three bears. He said that was very interesting.

On her way to school – she had been at school a couple of terms – Dinah told her friend about the three bears. Her friend said she had had *four* bears in her bed one time.

At school Dinah drew a picture of the three bears in her News Book. Her teacher, Mrs Hicks, said it was very nice dear. Dinah read her reading book to Mrs Hicks and did some writing. When the flowers got knocked over, she fetched the mop.

The school dinner was shepherd's pie, peas and gravy; sponge-cake and pineapple jelly.

After school Dinah went to play and have tea at her friend's house. They found a caterpillar in the garden. They made a home for it with dock leaves in a baby-food tin.

At half-past five Dinah came home. She fed her goldfish and watched TV for a while. She rode her bicycle along the pavement in front of the house.

When bedtime came, Dinah Price kissed her mum and dad goodnight, kissed her Uncle Jim too, who had called in for a visit, stroked the dog, climbed the stairs, went into her room – and found a wicked witch in her bed.

This witch was dressed all in black. She had a tall black hat on her head. There was a pair of black buttoned boots on the bedside rug. The witch's nose was large and had a wart on it. Her broomstick was propped up in a corner of the room. There was no sign of a cat.

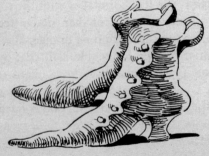

Dinah Price looked at the wicked witch and shivered in her nightie. She knew a bit about witches. Only last week her teacher, Mrs Hicks, had told them a story about a witch. This witch used to catch little children and fatten them up in a kind of birdcage. Later on she would bake them in a pie, given the chance.

The wicked witch looked at Dinah Price and scowled. 'You're a skinny little thing, ain't you?'

'Don't be rude,' said Dinah.

'Don't *you* be rude,' said the witch. She pulled the bedclothes up under her chin. Dinah noticed it had a few whiskers on it.

'You'd better mind your manners, little lady. I could turn you into a tin of beans.'

'My Uncle Jim is downstairs,' said Dinah. 'He is a hunter. He has got a gun.'

The wicked witch sniffed and pretended not to care. Even so, Dinah could see a worried look in her eyes. The truth is, Dinah's Uncle Jim was a bus driver, but the witch was not to know that.

The wicked witch peered at Dinah from beneath the brim of her hat. The hat had tilted forward a little over one eye. It cast a shadow on the wall. 'How about a story, then? They say y'get good stories hereabouts.'

'Who told you that?'

'Never you mind,' said the witch. She sniffed again. 'Come on – I haven't heard a story in weeks.'

Dinah Price thought for a minute. 'If I did tell you a story, would you promise to go home then – to your own bed?'

'Depends,' said the witch. 'It would need to be good.'

'It would be!'

'None of this "wicked witch" business.'

'No!'

'Right,' said the witch. 'It's a promise.' She snuggled further down the bed. Her long greenish fingers clutched the bedclothes either side of her chin. 'Come on – let's be having it.'

So Dinah Price pulled up her stool, picked up a book and began to read. 'Once upon a time there was –'

'Are you reading this or making it up?'

'Never you mind,' said Dinah, although the truth is she *was* making it up – as she had with the three bears.

'Manners, manners!' The witch pointed a finger at Dinah. 'I could turn you into a hole in the road.'

'Once upon a time,' said Dinah, 'there was a wicked . . . er, wonderful witch!'

'That's more like it,' said the witch.

'She was very beautiful, this witch – very beautiful. She had a beautiful black dress and hat, beautiful black hair and fingernails, and a very pretty wart on the end of her nose. Her name was . . .'

'Esmerelda!' said the witch. The witch's own name was not Esmerelda, but she had always wanted it to be.

'Esmerelda, that's it. Well, one day Esmerelda the witch was at home in her house in the middle of a wood.'

'What sort of house?'

'It was a neat little house,' said Dinah. 'It had a red roof, yellow curtains and roses round the door.'

'And a little white fence,' said the witch. 'You forgot that. And a rockery.'

'Yes. Well, there was the witch, and what she was doing was practising a few spells. She practised a spell for doing the washing-up, and a spell for making the beds, and ... all kinds of spells like that. Anyway, suddenly she heard a noise outside and looked to see what it was. It was a horrid, naughty, little boy. He was rattling a stick along the garden fence –'

'My beautiful little fence!' shouted the witch.

'– and whistling through his teeth. So Esmerelda thought for a minute, and said to herself, "I cannot stand for this. I'm going to teach that boy a lesson. What I'm going to do is –"'

'Cook him in a pie and eat him up!' shouted the witch.

'Er, well ...'

'That'll teach him!'

Dinah Price thought for a minute. She was not too happy with the way the story was going. She said, 'Well, anyway, first Esmerelda had to catch the horrid boy and –'

'Easy-peasy,' said the witch. 'She just jumped out and grabbed him. "Gotcha!" she said.'

Dinah paused again. She could feel the story slipping away from her. 'So then Esmerelda carried the boy back into the house and put him –'

'In a pie!' shouted the witch.

'And put him in a birdcage,' said Dinah, firmly; 'a big one, that she had hanging up in her kitchen. Because that horrid, naughty, little boy was also a skinny, naughty, little boy. He needed fattening up.'

'Ah – good thinking,' said the witch.

'So after that Esmerelda made lots of nice things and fed them to the boy to fatten him up. There was

21

fish-fingers, and baked beans on toast, and steak and kidney pie and chips, and treacle tart and custard, and chocolate cake; also there was orange squash and a few Smarties. Now this boy, besides being little, naughty and horrid, was also cheeky and brave.'

'Was he?' said the witch.

'Yes. So he ate up all these things without batting an eyelid, and afterwards sat in the birdcage whistling once more through his teeth.'

'Like a canary!' said the witch.

'Yes. And after that he even rattled his stick along the bars of the cage.'

'He's a pest, that boy,' said the witch.

'Well, Esmerelda kept feeding the boy up, day after day, and he kept eating and drinking everything he was given, and whistling through his teeth, and rattling his stick along the bars of the cage; but the funny thing was' – at this point Dinah had an idea for saving the boy – 'the funny thing was, he never got any fatter.'

The witch, however, was ready for her. 'Yes, he did. He got fatter all the time: fatter and fatter!'

'All right then, he got fatter. Fatter and fatter and fatter! So fat he couldn't whistle any more or rattle his stick along the bars of the cage.'

'I should have took that stick off him,' said the witch.

'So fat' – here Dinah had another idea – 'so fat that Esmerelda couldn't get him out of the cage.'

'Yes, she could,' said the witch. 'She smashed it open with an axe.'

'It was made out of iron.'

'Cut it with a hacksaw!' shouted the witch.

'She hadn't got one.'

'Pulled it to pieces with her bare hands!' screamed the witch.

By this time the witch was sitting bolt upright in the bed. Her hat had fallen off. Her hair was sticking out like straw. 'What's going on here? I'm offering a good story, and all I get is aggravation.'

'You keep butting in, that's the trouble,' said Dinah. 'Whose story is it, anyway?'

'That's what I want to know!' The witch leant over the side of the bed. She picked up her hat, which was on the floor.

At that moment a voice called up in an angry whisper from the hall. 'Dinah! You stop that noise and go to sleep, do you hear?' It was Dinah's mum. 'You wake little Maurice up and there'll be trouble.' Then there was the sound of a door closing and – after that – silence.

Dinah looked at the wicked witch and the wicked witch looked at Dinah. Both had guilty expressions on their faces.

'Who's little Maurice?' said the witch.

'My baby brother,' said Dinah. 'He's in the other room.'

'Ah!' The witch stared closely at her hat. She wiped it on the sleeve of her dress and put it on. She drummed with her fingers against the side of the bed.

'So anyway, what happened – in this story of mine?'

'What happened –' said Dinah. 'No more shouting now – what happened was . . . just then a handsome prince came riding by –'

'And *he* had a hacksaw!'

'No, he didn't. He stopped at the witch's house for a drink of water. While he was drinking –' now Dinah had a third idea. 'While he was drinking, he looked at Esmerelda. He looked at her beautiful black dress and hat, her beautiful black hair and fingernails, and the pretty little wart on the end of her nose. He said to himself, "Who is this woman? She must be the fairest in the land!"'

The wicked witch pulled the bedclothes up once more under her chin. A blush appeared on her otherwise greenish cheeks. She looked embarrassed, but pleased too. She showed no sign of butting in.

'So Esmerelda invited the prince to stay for tea, which he did. They had egg and tomato sandwiches, bakewell tart, home-made lemonade and a few peanuts. The prince offered to help with the washing-up, but Esmerelda wouldn't let him into the kitchen. Then after that they went for a walk in the woods and the prince asked Esmerelda to marry him.'

'Is there a picture of him there?' whispered the witch.

Dinah turned the pages of her book. 'No. You'll have to imagine him for yourself.'

'I can do that . . . keep going.'

'So anyway, the prince asked Esmerelda to marry him. "You are the fairest in the land," he said.'

'What did *she* say?' said the witch.

'She said, "Oh, your Highness, I am but a humble witch. I do not deserve –"'

'But she said *yes* though,' said the witch, beginning to scowl once more.

'She said yes,' said Dinah. 'After that she packed her nightie, face-flannel and toothbrush in a little bag and rode away on the prince's horse to his castle in a far country.'

'And lived happily ever after,' whispered the witch.

'That's it,' said Dinah, and she closed her book. 'The End.'

The wicked witch heaved a deep sigh and sat up in the bed. It was darker in the room now. Her hat no longer cast its shadow on the wall. In the tree outside the window, birds were twittering. From farther off came the chimes of an ice-cream van.

The witch got out of the bed. She reached for her button boots and put them on. 'That story was all right; got better as it went along.' She collected her broomstick and went over to the window. She gazed out. 'Is this your garden down here?'

'Yes,' said Dinah.

'The hedge wants cutting.'

Dinah put her book on the bedside table and joined the witch at the window. 'Are you going home now – to your own house and your own bed?'

'No, I'll probably fly around for a bit,' said the witch. 'Witches work nights, you know.' She climbed out onto the window ledge. 'By the way, what became of that boy? That little pest with the stick?'

'Oh, he just stayed in the birdcage for a while,' said Dinah, 'whistling to himself, till he got thinner and thinner and slipped out through the bars.'

The wicked witch dangled her bony legs over the window ledge and clutched the broom between her knees. 'I think I'll keep an eye open for that boy,' she said.

After that she said goodbye to Dinah Price, flew off over the gardens and garages, and disappeared into the blue and purple haze above the allotments.

Dinah watched her go. She shut the window and pulled the curtains across. She got into the bed – still warm from the witch – turned over on her side, and slept until morning.

3

The Clockwork Mouse

The next day Dinah Price got up, got dressed and had her breakfast. She had cornflakes with the top of the milk on them, a piece of bread-and-butter dipped in her dad's boiled egg, a cup of tea and an orange. She told her dad about the wicked witch. He said that was very interesting. Her mum said it was very interesting too. Now we know what all the noise was, she said.

On her way to school Dinah told her friend about the wicked witch. Her friend said she had had a wicked *wizard* in her bed one time.

At school Dinah made a model of the witch out of an egg-box. Her teacher, Mrs Hicks, said it was very nice dear. She put it on the Interest Table with a label saying what it was and who had made it.

The school dinner was steak and kidney pie, carrots and gravy; treacle tart and custard.

In the afternoon a boy in Dinah's class brought some frogs to school. They were baby frogs. He had them in a little plastic bucket. Mrs Hicks let everybody see the frogs. Some of the children wrote about them in their News Books. When the bucket got knocked over, Dinah's friend fetched the mop.

After school Dinah went to the shop for her mum. She fetched a bag of sugar, a packet of frozen peas and a lolly. She had her tea and played with her baby brother in the garden. She wanted to play with her big brother in the park; but he was going with his friends and wouldn't take her.

When bedtime came, Dinah Price kissed her mum and dad goodnight, asked if she could watch a teeny bit of the programme they were watching, watched a bit of it, climbed the stairs, went into her room – and found a cat in her bed.

This cat was sitting up in the bed like a human being. He was turning the key in a clockwork mouse. He had a hat with a feather in it beside him on the bed – and a violin-case.

Dinah sat down on her stool.

> '*Hey diddle diddle,*
> *The cat and the fiddle,*'

she said. 'Is that you?'

'Used to be,' said the cat. 'But I have since gone on to

better things.' He smoothed the bedclothes and released the mouse. With occasional stops and starts, it scuttled round in a circle. From time to time the cat batted it with his paw. 'There's not much of a part for an ambitious cat in *Hey Diddle Diddle*, you know.'

'I never thought of that,' said Dinah.

'The dish and the spoon have the best of it – well, the dish does.' The cat reached for the mouse and began rewinding it. 'There again,

> *Ding dong bell,*
> *Pussy's in the well*

is even worse!'

'Were you the pussy in the well as well?'

'In earlier years,' said the cat; 'though I was little more than a kitten then.'

'Have you been lots of cats?'

'Lots – bit parts mostly; though lately, as I say, things are looking up.' Once more the cat released the mouse. Dinah watched it go bumpily over the bedclothes. The cat watched Dinah.

'Do you like that mouse?'

'Yes,' said Dinah.

'Right – to business. Do you want to buy it?'

'I haven't got any money,' Dinah said.

'I guessed as much. Do you want to swop for it?'

Dinah knew she was not supposed to swop for things. She sometimes got into trouble for that. All the same she said, 'What could I swop?'

'Well . . .' The cat glanced casually round the room. 'In this part I have now, what I'm most in need of . . . is a fish.'

Dinah followed the direction of the cat's gaze. He

was looking at the goldfish tank.

'Oh, no – not the goldfish! Besides, I have just thought, I'm not supposed to swop for things.'

'That's too bad.' The cat opened the violin-case, took out a second clockwork mouse and set it going after the first. 'Could I tempt you with two of them?'

'Er . . . no,' said Dinah.

'Pity.' The cat leant forward and batted one of the mice. 'Not to worry; I'll think of something.'

For a moment there was silence. Dinah too was thinking. She said, 'Would you really eat those goldfish, if you could – *raw*?'

'No,' the cat shook his head. 'I prefer blackbirds baked in a pie. No, the fish isn't for me, it's for the king. You see, in this part I have, I need –'

'What *is* the part?' said Dinah.

And the cat said, 'Guess!'

So then Dinah tried to guess what part the cat was playing.

'I don't think you're a witch's cat,' she said. 'You don't act like one. You aren't the crooked cat the crooked man bought with his crooked sixpence either.'

'I'm glad of that,' said the cat.

'What others are there? I know – maybe you're the one in *The Owl and the Pussy Cat*.

The owl and the pussy cat went to sea
In a beautiful pea-green boat.'

'No,' said the cat. 'That's not me. I remember being offered the part, but I turned it down. Who wants to marry an owl?'

'I never thought of that,' said Dinah.

Once more there was silence. Dinah tried to think of other cats she had heard of. The one in her bed twiddled with his whiskers and gazed thoughtfully around him. Through the open window came the sound of a car-door slamming. There was the faint 'snip-snip' of garden shears, which was Dinah's mum cutting the hedge.

The cat said, 'Look here, since we're short of time, I'll give you a clue.' He reached for the hat with the feather in it, and with a flourish placed it on his head. 'Any good?'

Dinah thought for a minute. 'No.'

'Right – here's another!'

With these words the cat stuck one of his back feet out at the side of the bed. And the foot, as perhaps Dinah should have guessed, had a boot on it.

'Oh,' said Dinah. 'Puss in Boots!'

'That's it – you got it!' The cat took his hat off again and batted the feather with his paw. 'Puss in Boots, sometimes called "The Master Cat". It's a star part, you see.'

'I do,' said Dinah.

'Oh, yes. So now you know why I need the fish.'

'Well, I have *heard* the story,' said Dinah. 'Mrs Hicks told it us. But I'm not sure I remember a fish being in it.'

'You should – the fish is crucial. You see, there's this

33

old miller and he dies and leaves his youngest son a cat.'

'I remember *that*,' said Dinah.

'Well, this young fellow is fed-up with only being left a cat. But, of course, it isn't any old cat, it's Puss in Boots. Anyway, Puss in Boots is very clever. He has this idea to make the youngest son rich. What he does is, he goes out, catches a fish and carries it to the king. He says it is a present for him from his master, the Lord Marquis of Carabas, which is a name he just made up, you see – for the youngest son.'

'I remember that as well,' Dinah said.

'Yes; what he says is –' At this point the cat leapt from the bed and struck a dramatic pose on the bedside rug. 'What he says is: "My Lord Marquis of Carabas, Your Majesty's most humble slave, craves your indulgence and with all due respects sends you this fish."'

The cat made a flourish with his hat and bowed low to Dinah. Then, pretending she was the king, he mimed the presentation of the fish to her.

Dinah mimed the acceptance of it – and clapped her hands. 'That's very good!'

'Oh, I know my lines.' The cat purred briefly and twiddled with his whiskers. 'Anyway, you remember the rest. Puss in Boots takes other gifts to the king and, this way and that, fixes it up for the youngest son to marry his daughter. Even gets him a castle too!'

'Yes,' said Dinah, 'I remember; and it's an ogre's castle, isn't it?'

'It is; that's the tricky bit. Still, it's in the script, so what can you do?' The cat gave each of his boots a tug. They had floppy tops and were rather big for him. 'Anyway, that's why I need the fish. No fish: no story. Trouble is, fishing's not a sport I'm any good at.'

Now the cat was getting ready to leave. He opened the violin-case and put the clockwork mice in it. Dinah wondered how many more he had in there.

The cat said, 'I've just thought – you never told me your name.'

'It's Dinah Price,' said Dinah.

'Well, Dinah Price, it's been a pleasure meeting you. If I wasn't so concerned about this fish, I'd stay and talk some more. You speak your lines very nicely.'

'Thank you,' said Dinah. She had never thought she was speaking 'lines' before.

The cat adjusted his hat in the dressing-table mirror. It was darker in the room now, but there was still light for him to see by. He said, 'This part seems to suit you. What other parts have you had?'

Dinah frowned. She had never thought she was playing 'a part' either. She said, 'I was in the school play at Christmas. It was the nativity.'

'Nativity? Is there a part for a cat in that?'

'Not really,' said Dinah. 'It's about the Baby Jesus.'

'Ah – and who were you?'

'I was the shepherd's little girl: *The shepherds watched their flocks by night*. I had to take him his supper wrapped in a cloth.'

'Did you have any lines?'

'Yes – but I don't remember them now.'

'I remember mine,' said the cat; 'every one of them – even the first.' He stepped over to the window, stood on the toy-box and peered out. 'Yes, my first lines were in *The Three Little Kittens*. You know, they lost their mittens and all that.'

'I know,' said Dinah.

'Let's see how did it go . . .?

> *Oh mother dear*
> *We sadly fear*
> *Our mittens we have lost!'*

And Dinah said,

> *'What – lost your mittens?*
> *You naughty kittens*
> *Then you shall have no pie!'*

And the cat said,

> *'Miao! Miao! Miao!'*

After that he looked out of the window again.

'Do you have far to go?' said Dinah.

'Not too far,' said the cat. 'I know a short cut.'

'Will you go down the drainpipe?'

'Not if I can help it.' Then the cat said, 'There's a woman out here trimming a hedge.'

'That's my mum,' said Dinah.

'There's a man in green overalls unpegging nappies from a line — and there's a dog watching him.'

'That's my dad and my dog.'

'Right,' said the cat. 'Should be clear downstairs then. Have you got a cat-door?'

'No,' said Dinah.

'Not to worry, maybe the kitchen window's open. I'll take a look.'

The cat left his hat and violin-case on the bed and stepped out of the room. Dinah remained on her stool. She leant forward and flicked at the handle of the violin-case. She thought about the cat being in bed with his boots on, and what her mum would say to that. She thought about the fish.

When the cat returned, he said, 'That's lucky — the back door's open!' He reached for his hat.

Dinah said, 'I've been thinking — about the fish. Wouldn't fish-fingers do?'

'Hardly,' said the cat.

'Well does it have to be a fish at all?'

'I suppose not. I think it was a rabbit in one version, which is no help to me. I can't catch them either.'

'What about a mouse then?'

'Might manage that,' said the cat; 'though I doubt if the king would thank me for it.'

Just then Dinah had an idea. 'What about a *clockwork* mouse? He'd thank you for that.'

'Do you think so?' The cat twiddled with his whiskers. 'It's not in the script. There again, neither were goldfish.'

(not) (me) (again)

'That's what I was going to say,' said Dinah.

'Yes . . .' The cat batted at the tasselled cord of Dinah's dressing-gown, which was hanging behind the door. 'You know, I believe you're on to something . . . I'll do it!'

With these words the cat once more removed a clockwork mouse from his violin-case. Then he bowed low to Dinah again and made a flourish with his hat. 'My Lord Marquis of Carabas, Your Majesty's most humble slave, craves your indulgence and with all due respects sends you this . . . clockwork mouse!'

And Dinah said, 'How very nice! How pretty! You must marry my daughter at once.'

'Not me,' said the cat. 'I'm the cat! What you say is –' He put out a paw. Reluctantly, Dinah handed back the mouse she'd been 'presented' with. 'What you say is –'

'Have you got lots of clockwork mice in there?' said Dinah.

'Lots,' said the cat. 'There's some sugar mice as well.'

'Really?'

'Yes – look! And chocolate ones.'

'So there is,' said Dinah.

'What else is there?' said the cat. 'Let's see, I've a mouse balloon in here, I seem to remember . . . mouse glove-puppet, pencil-sharpener, party-squeaker. Only thing I'm short of is a violin.'

The cat put his hat on again and closed the violin-case. 'Anyway, I'd best be off. I might just reach the palace before the king has his supper.' He went over to the window. 'Shall I shut this window and pull the curtains across?'

'Yes, please,' said Dinah.

'Right. Now then, you get into bed and I'll tuck you in.'

Dinah did as she was told. It was really quite dark in the room now. The cat was no more than a shadow. Only his eyes gleamed.

The cat said, 'One last thing.' He came up close to Dinah. 'What's your favourite: sugar or chocolate?'

'Chocolate – no, sugar!' Dinah said.

After that the cat placed into Dinah's hand a sugar mouse, said thank-you-very-much-for-all-your-help, closed the door, went down the stairs, out of the house, up the street – and away.

Dinah Price lay in the bed and sucked her sugar mouse. When it got small, she tucked it in her cheek to make it last. When it was gone, she suddenly wished she'd kept it. 'I could have shown it to my friend,' she said to herself.

After that she closed her eyes – and slept till morning.

4

The Accident Book

The next day Dinah Price got up, got dressed and had her breakfast. She had cornflakes but no top of the milk because there was none left. There were no oranges either, so she had half a banana. Dinah wanted to tell her dad about Puss in Boots, but he was late for work and had to dash. Her mum was helping him. Her big brother was finishing some homework he should have done the night before. So Dinah told her baby brother instead. He was in his high-chair, slopping his breakfast about. He listened attentively, sucked his spoon and said, 'Pussy Boo!'

At school Dinah read her reading book to Mrs Hicks and did six sums. She drew a picture of Puss in Boots climbing a hill to the king's palace. Her friend helped her to colour it in. Her friend showed Dinah a wobbly tooth she had. It was getting wobblier. She showed it to another girl too, and some boys and Mrs Hicks and the caretaker.

At dinnertime Dinah fell down in the playground. She grazed her knee. The dinner-lady put a plaster on it, and wrote her name in the Accident Book. She showed it to Dinah.

In the afternoon Mrs Hicks's class went into the hall. They watched a play which the fourth years had made up. It was about pirates mostly. The pirates had sword-fights with school rulers, and rescued each other from the P.E. apparatus. When the play was over, Mrs Hicks said they deserved a clap. Dinah clapped so hard, her hands stung. All the children clapped for a long time. Mrs Hicks had to tell them to stop.

After school Dinah told her mum about getting her name in the Accident Book. Her mum took the plaster off and put a clean one on. In the bath, Dinah kept her knee above the water like a little island.

When bedtime came, she kissed her mum and dad goodnight, kissed her big brother too, although he kept ducking out of the way, stroked the dog, climbed the stairs, went into her room – and found Sleeping Beauty in her bed.

Sleeping Beauty was sitting up in the bed, yawning hugely and looking at herself in a powder-compact mirror. Spread out in front of her were various lipsticks, pots of face cream, scent-sprays, tubes of this and that, tweezers, nail files, a silver comb and a pair of silver-backed brushes. Also there was a small suitcase with a coat of arms on it.

Dinah Price looked at Sleeping Beauty. She was wearing a frilly pink nightdress and a fluffy pink bed-jacket. Her hair was fluffy and blonde; her cheeks, peach-coloured. She had a rose-bud mouth and the beginnings of a double-chin. Under the bed, Dinah noticed, there was a pair of slippers. These were pink too, with fluffy pompoms.

Sleeping Beauty did not look at Dinah, but continued to look at herself in the mirror. She smoothed her eyebrows with a wet finger.

Dinah said, 'Are you –'

'Sh!' said Sleeping Beauty. 'I am concentrating here.' She applied a dab of powder to her cheek. 'When a person is as beautiful as I – I am Sleeping Beauty, you know ... When a person ...' She yawned once more

I'm so beautiful...

and did not finish what she was saying.

Dinah went up to the bed and reached for a scent-spray. 'Can I have a go with –'

'Hands off, little child.' Sleeping Beauty had a slow and sleepy way of speaking. 'I need that spray. You, on the other hand, are too young for such things.' For the first time Sleeping Beauty was looking at Dinah. 'Too young . . . and hardly beautiful enough.'

Dinah reached for a lipstick. 'What about –'

'Put it down.'

Dinah reached for the silver comb.

'No.' Sleeping Beauty made a circle with her arms to fend Dinah off. 'These things belong to me.'

'Well, this bed belongs to me,' said Dinah, 'but you're in it.'

'That is altogether different,' said Sleeping Beauty. She had finished 'dolling herself up', as Dinah's grandma would have said, and was beginning to snuggle under the bedclothes. 'I am Sleeping Beauty, you know . . .' She yawned and closed her eyes. 'When a person is as beautiful as I . . .'

Dinah Price sat on her stool and thought for a minute. She thought of getting into the bed with Sleeping Beauty and gradually pushing her out. But, even though it was her own bed, she couldn't. She felt shy. Sometimes she got into bed with her mum and dad and pushed *them* out; but that was altogether different. Then Dinah had another idea.

'Listen!' She gave Sleeping Beauty a shake. 'I am going to tell you a story. After that you will get out of the bed and I will get into it. Then you will go home to your *own* bed, and I will go to sleep.'

'I am . . . (yawn) . . . going to sleep now,' said

Sleeping Beauty. She turned over on her side. Some of the pots and jars clinked together.

'No, you're not,' said Dinah. 'Here's the story – it's a good one. Listen!'

And this is the story she told.

'Once upon a time there was a king and queen who wanted very much to have a baby. Well, one day they did. So then there was a great feast and everybody was invited, including the fairies – only they forgot one fairy.' Dinah paused for breath. 'Then the fairy they forgot put an evil spell on the baby, saying she would prick her finger with a needle and go to sleep for a hundred years.'

'One moment, little child.' Sleeping Beauty opened her eyes. 'That is not altogether correct. Furthermore, you are leaving the best bits out.'

'I am in a hurry,' said Dinah. 'I have to go to sleep myself. I will get into trouble if I don't.'

'But you didn't tell about the gifts,' said Sleeping Beauty. 'The other fairies gave me gifts. They said I would be the most beautiful person in the world.' Sleeping Beauty sighed complacently. 'And have the

wit of an angel, and admirable grace in everything I did; dance perfectly ... sing like a ... (yawn) ... nightingale ... play upon all kinds of instruments to the utmost ...' Sleeping Beauty closed her eyes. She did not finish what she was saying.

'Well, anyway,' said Dinah, 'after that the king passed a law saying there must be no needles anywhere in his kingdom. All the same, one old lady didn't hear about the law, and sixteen years later she was sitting up in a tower sewing and Sleeping Beauty came in and said what is this dear little thing and the old lady said it was a needle and Sleeping Beauty pricked her finger and fell down on the floor.'

'Tragic,' murmured Sleeping Beauty.

'Then the king and queen came in –' Dinah paused and glanced slyly at Sleeping Beauty; '– and the queen put a plaster on the finger.' ('A plaster?' said Sleeping Beauty.) 'And the king wrote her name in the Accident Book.'

'Accident Book?' Once more Sleeping Beauty opened her eyes. 'I suspect you are making a mockery of this story, little child.'

'Well, after that the king and queen put Sleeping Beauty in her own bed – where she belonged – and she slept for a hundred years till the prince came by who was going to kiss her and wake her up.'

'This is the part I like,' said Sleeping Beauty. She was beginning to doze again.

'When the prince came, he looked at Sleeping Beauty, who was lying there with all her best clothes on and all her powder-compacts and scent-sprays around her.' At this point Dinah reached for a scent-spray and, unobserved by Sleeping Beauty, sprayed herself a little behind each ear, as she had seen her mother do. 'He looked at her and said to himself, "I cannot kiss this woman; her hair is too frizzy."'

'What?' said Sleeping Beauty.

'"Her nose is too big."'

Sleeping Beauty sat bolt upright in the bed.

'"And she has got a double-chin!"'

'Stop that!' said Sleeping Beauty. 'He never said those things.' She was as wide awake as she had been all evening. 'What happened was, I said – when he woke me up, which he did – I said, "Is it you, my prince? You have waited a great while."'

'I have waited a great while,' said Dinah. 'My feet are freezing.'

'And the prince was charmed with these words and much more with the manner they were spoken in and he said he loved me better than he loved himself.'

'I don't believe that.' Dinah reached for a lipstick. 'You're making it up.'

'Making it up? I am not making it up. It is the truth. I was there!'

Sleeping Beauty scooped the lipstick out of Dinah's reach. 'Nevertheless, I shall not argue with you, dreadful child! I do not have to stand for this.'

'You're lying down,' said Dinah.

'I shall return to my own abode.' Sleeping Beauty put the lipstick in the suitcase. She began putting the other things in as well.

'Are you going home?' said Dinah.

Sleeping Beauty did not reply, but muttered to herself, 'No respect for history.' There was a sulky expression on her rose-bud mouth. 'When a person is as beautiful as I . . .'

The moment her packing was finished, Sleeping Beauty flounced from the bed and put her slippers on. 'How do I get out of here?'

'How did you get in?' said Dinah.

'I don't remember.'

'Down the drainpipe, then,' Dinah said.

Dinah Price and Sleeping Beauty crossed to the window and looked out. It was getting dark. A blue and purple haze was gathering along the edge of the sky above the allotments. A darker smudge of smoke rose from a bonfire in the next-door neighbour's garden. Higher in the sky, the white trail of an aeroplane was stretching out in one direction, dissolving in the other.

Dinah and Sleeping Beauty looked down.

'There's the drainpipe,' Dinah said. 'Can you manage?'

Sleeping Beauty clambered out onto the ledge. 'Easily.' She took hold of the drainpipe. 'I have admirable . . . (yawn) . . . grace in everything I do.'

After that she began to descend. She had the handle of the little suitcase clenched between her teeth.

'What if she yawns now?' thought Dinah.

Sleeping Beauty reached the ground. One of her slippers had dropped off on the way and got there ahead of her. She put it on and gazed about. Then, patting her hair in place, she set off down the garden and very soon disappeared among the rhododendron bushes.

Dinah Price watched her go. She shut the window, pulled the curtains across and got into bed. It was still warm and perfumed from the Sleeping Beauty. 'I will tell my friend about this tomorrow,' Dinah said to herself. Then she said, 'No, I won't – it's Saturday.' Shortly after that she closed her eyes, turned over on her side – and slept till morning.

5

Wilfred

The next day Dinah Price got up, put her slippers on and went into her mum and dad's room. Because it was Saturday, they were still in bed. Her baby brother was in the bed too; he was bouncing in it. Dinah sat on the bed and told her mum and dad about Sleeping Beauty. But the baby's bouncing was distracting them. Also, they were arguing, as usual, about which of them should fetch the tea; and so they didn't listen.

After breakfast Dinah went shopping with her mum and dad. Her baby brother was being looked after by a neighbour. Her big brother was playing football with his friends. In town Dinah bought some ants' eggs for her goldfish. Outside the Co-op she saw her teacher, Mrs Hicks. Mrs Hicks said hallo, and Dinah felt quite shy.

When the shopping was finished, Dinah and her mum and dad had lunch at a café. It was self-service. Dinah had bacon and sausage, chips and peas, apple crumble, custard and a cup of tea.

In the afternoon Dinah's Uncle Jim came round with his motor-bike. Dinah's dad helped him to take it to bits on the drive. When she got the chance, Dinah told Uncle Jim about Sleeping Beauty. Uncle Jim said he had a sleeping beauty of his own – Dinah's Auntie Annie. She would sleep for *two* hundred years if you let her, he said.

Before tea Dinah went with her dad and her big brother to take the dog for a walk. They went into the park. Dinah's dad let the dog off the lead and had trouble getting him back. Dinah and her brother had a

go on the swings. They watched two girls flying a kite.

When bedtime came, Dinah Price kissed her mum and dad goodnight, kissed her Uncle Jim too, who was still there and had oil on his nose, climbed the stairs, went into her room – and found a wolf in her bed.

This wolf lay in the bed with the bedclothes up to his chin. His front paws rested on the eiderdown. He had an old lady's nightcap on his head, with one wolfish ear sticking out. There was a smile of sorts on his wolfish face.

Dinah remained near the door with her hand on the door-knob, and looked at the wolf. She knew a bit about wolves. There was the wolf that Red Riding Hood had had trouble with when she went to visit her grandma. There was another one – or was it the same one? – who had tried to get the three little pigs out of their three little houses. Dinah comforted herself with the thought that the wolf had not triumphed in either case. Wolves were the *losers* in the stories she knew.

The wolf lay in the bed and looked craftily at Dinah. 'Come in, my dear, come in.' He spoke in an unconvincing squeaky voice. 'Have you brought a custard pie and a little pot of butter for your old grandma?'

'Of course not,' said Dinah. 'You are not my old grandma. You are not anybody's old grandma. You are a wolf.'

'Quite so,' said the wolf in his normal voice. He sat up in bed and removed his grandma's cap, 'On the other hand, it seemed worth a try.'

'I am not Red Riding Hood either. My name is Dinah Price.'

'Is that a fact? Well, do not get uppity with me,

Dinah Price, or I might eat y'up. I might eat y'up anyway.'

'My Uncle Jim is downstairs,' said Dinah. 'He is a hunter. He has got a gun.'

'I might eat him up as well.' The ease with which Dinah had spotted his disguise had put the wolf in a bad mood.

Dinah made an effort to change the subject. 'Would you, er . . . would you like it if I told you a story?'

'A story?' said the wolf. 'What for?'

'Well, you see, I tell you a story, and you listen, and then you go home – to your own house and your own bed.'

'Why should I do that?' said the wolf. And he said, 'What's it about?'

Dinah thought for a minute. She ventured a step or two towards the bed. 'It's about a good little wolf, who lived with his mum and dad and his big brother and his baby brother on the edge of a wood. You see, one day –'

'What was his name?' said the wolf.

'What's your name?'

'Er . . . Wilfred,' said the wolf.

'That was his name –
Wilfred! Well, one day
Wilfred's mummy gave him
some nice lamb chops in a
little basket to take to his
poor old grandma, who lived
in a cottage in the middle of
the wood. It was a neat
little cottage. It had a red
roof, yellow curtains and roses –'

'You can skip all that,' said the wolf.

'Yes . . . So, anyway, Wilfred put his hat and coat on and set off to his grandma's cottage. He picked a few flowers for his grandma on the way, and whistled a tune to himself called . . . *The Teddy Bears' Picnic*.'

'Never heard of it,' said the wolf. Despite his grumpy remarks, he was beginning to attend to the story and making himself more comfortable in the bed.

'All of a sudden, Wilfred the wolf met a naughty little girl named Red Riding Hood. She wanted to get his lamb chops off him and have them for herself. Well —'

'Wait a minute.' The wolf was frowning. 'In this story of yours, does the wolf get to eat Red Riding Hood up, and her grandma?'

'*Her* grandma isn't in the story.'

'*And* her grandma,' said the wolf. 'And live happily ever after?'

'Well, not really.'

'Not interested then,' said the wolf. 'I only like stories with happy endings where the wolf gets to eat everybody.'

'I never heard of any stories like that.'

'That shows how little *you* know.' The wolf turned over on his side to face the wall. He appeared to be sulking.

'In the ones I know, a hunter or a wood-cutter or somebody always comes at the last minute and, er . . . stops the wolf,' said Dinah tactfully.

'Yes, well there's other versions,' said the wolf over his shoulder. 'Lots of 'em.'

Dinah took a step nearer the bed. She was standing now at the foot of it. 'Such as?'

'Such as?' The wolf turned to face her. 'Such as where the wolf just gets to eat Red Riding Hood up and that's the end of it! That's the oldest version, if you only knew it. Or where he eats her, her grandma, the wood-cutter, and four or five others who came along, poked their noses in and wished they hadn't. That's the one our mother used to tell us.'

The wolf sat up in the bed and toyed with his grandma's cap. 'Yes, there's lots of versions. I even heard of one where the wolf had a motor-bike.'

'My Uncle Jim has a motor-bike,' said Dinah.

'You said he was a hunter.'

'So he is. He's a hunter – with a motor-bike.'

Then Dinah said, 'What about *The Wolf and the Three Little Pigs*? Are there lots of versions of that?'

'I couldn't say,' said the wolf. 'That's some other wolf.'

'It's where the wolf says, "I'll huff and I'll puff and I'll blow your house in!"'

'All right, all right!' The wolf's temper seemed to be worsening. 'I didn't say I hadn't *heard* the story.'

'Then there's the song,' said Dinah. 'You know: *Who's Afraid of the Big Bad Wolf?*'

'I'm not musical,' said the wolf.

'It goes:

> *Who's afraid of the big bad wolf,*
> *The big bad wolf,*
> *The big bad wolf?*
> *Who's afraid of the big bad wolf?*
> *Tra la la la la!'*

The wolf scowled. '*Tra la la la la* – that's a weak line.' And he said, 'Anyway, what about this story you were telling?'

'You said you weren't interested,' said Dinah.

'I've changed my mind; if it's either that or *Tra la la la la*. Besides, I've just thought of something.' The wolf seemed suddenly to be cheering up. 'Why don't we just have the best part of the story? You know: where Red Riding Hood comes to her grandma's cottage, and her grandma is, well, *under* the bed, say tied up, and the wolf is in the bed cunningly disguised' – the wolf put his grandma's cap on – 'cunningly disguised as the grandma.'

'What about little Wilfred?' said Dinah.

'Forget little Wilfred. Now then, let's do it like this!' The wolf was definitely cheering up. 'You be Red Riding Hood and I'll be the wolf.'

'You *are* the wolf,' said Dinah.

'Then you say, "O Grandma, what big ears you've got." And I say –'

'I'm not sure about this,' said Dinah.

'Come on – be a sport!'

'Well, if the proper grandma really is only tied up under the bed –'

'She is! She hasn't got a scratch.'

'And if you promise to go home afterwards – to your own bed.'

'I promise – cross my heart and hope to die!'

'Well . . .'

'That's the ticket!' The wolf pulled the bedclothes up to his chin and placed his front paws on the eiderdown. 'Now, you come in with your little basket and – what can you use for a basket?'

'I've got a basket,' said Dinah. 'It's one I had my Easter egg in.' She opened her wardrobe and took out a small raffia basket.

'That'll do. So you come in with your basket and sit on the stool.'

Hesitantly, Dinah sat on the stool.

'Then you say . . .'

'Oh Grandma, what big ears you've got,' said Dinah.

'That's it. And I say' – once more the wolf assumed his squeaky voice – 'all the better to hear you with, my dear.'

'Oh Grandma, what big eyes you've got!' said Dinah. She spoke now with more expression. She was getting into the part.

And the wolf said, 'All the better to see you with, my dear.'

'Oh Grandma –' Dinah paused. There was a slight noise on the landing: a creaking stair; the bathroom door closing. 'Oh Grandma, what big . . . what big . . .'

'Come on, come on!' said the wolf.

'What big . . . teeth you've got!' said Dinah.

'All the better to eat you with, my dear!' At this point, perhaps carried away by the part *he* was playing, the wolf threw back the bedclothes and made as if to

leap on Dinah, and – who knows? – gobble her up.

'Help, help!' shouted Dinah.

And at *that* point a voice on the landing called out: 'Is everything all right?'

'It's Uncle Jim!' said Dinah.

Quick as a flash, the wolf leapt from the bed and dived into the wardrobe. He was only just in time. For then the bedroom door opened and Uncle Jim stuck his head in. 'Is everything all right?'

'Well,' said Dinah. 'I have got a wolf in my wardrobe.'

'Ah!' said Uncle Jim. He looked across the darkening room to the wardrobe. Its door was shut. The wolf had closed it behind him. 'Which one is it: *Red Riding Hood* or *Three Little Pigs*?'

'*Red Riding Hood*,' said Dinah.

'Ah!' said Uncle Jim. 'So what would you like me to do – shoot him?'

Dinah sat on her bed and thought for a minute. 'I'm not sure.'

'Or I could run him over, maybe – with my motor-bike.'

'It depends,' Dinah raised her voice. 'It depends – *how he behaves himself*!'

'Ah!' said Uncle Jim. He advanced into the room. 'Nice place you've got here.' He took a yoyo from the toy-box, had a go with it and put it back. After that he whistled briefly and glanced out of the window. Then he said, 'Well, I suppose you'll want to be getting to sleep now.'

Dinah did not reply. She was uncertain what to say.

All the same, she got into the bed and allowed herself to be tucked in. Uncle Jim gave her a kiss on the top of her head. He smelled of petrol, she noticed, and had a pencil behind his ear.

On his way out Uncle Jim said, 'I'll leave the door open a little. If that wolf starts acting up again, just call.' Then he was gone.

Dinah Price lay in the bed – and waited. She could hear the birds twittering in the tree outside the window, and an ambulance siren a long way off. She could hear her own breathing, her own heart beating. She could hear – just faintly – the jangling of coat-hangers in the wardrobe.

At last the wolf emerged, clutching his grandma's cap in one paw and looking worried. He scowled at Dinah and stepped over to the window. It was open, but he opened it further.

Dinah said, 'Are you going home now, Wilfred?'

'Less of the Wilfred,' said the wolf. He lowered his voice to a whisper. 'Do not get uppity with me, little lady. I might still eat y'up.'

'But are you going, all the same?'

'Definitely,' said the wolf. And to himself added, 'Run over by a motor-bike – that's a *new* version!'

After that he leapt up on to the window ledge, out into the tree, down on to the dewy grass – and away.

Dinah slipped out of bed and shut the window behind him. She looked out into the garden, but already the wolf had disappeared. A heavy bee blundered against the window and made her jump. She pulled the curtains across and got into bed.

Dinah Price lay in the bed and stared up at the ceiling. After a while she closed her eyes, turned over on her side – and slept till morning.

6

Captain Dynamite Simon

The next day Dinah Price got up, put her slippers on and went down to the kitchen. It was Sunday. Her big brother was already there. He was eating a bowl of shredded wheat and watching the birds on the lawn outside the window. Dinah had a bowl of cornflakes with the top of the milk on them. She helped her brother to make breakfast in bed for their mum and dad. They made tea and toast and carried it upstairs on two trays. Dinah's mum and dad asked her about the wolf in her wardrobe, which Uncle Jim had told them about. Dinah said he was the *Red Riding Hood* wolf, not the *Three Little Pigs* wolf; he didn't like *Who's Afraid of the Big Bad Wolf?* because he wasn't musical and his name was Wilfred.

During the morning Dinah helped her dad to clean the car. A procession went by in the street. It was the Salvation Army. They stopped at the corner and played *There is a Green Hill Far Away* and *Onward Christian Soldiers*. Dinah's dad gave her 10p to put in the collection tin.

In the afternoon Dinah and her family went for a picnic by the reservoir. Dinah's mum parked the car in a car park with a log fence round it. She gave Dinah 20p to give to the attendant.

Dinah Price sat with her family by the reservoir. She watched people fishing and flying kites. Her dad found a buttercup. He held it under her chin to see if she liked butter. Dinah held it under his chin, and her mum's chin, and her brothers' chins to see if they did. Dinah's mum let the dog off his lead and had trouble getting him back. Then it rained.

Dinah and her family – and the dog – ate their picnic in the car. They had egg sandwiches, sardine sandwiches, sausage rolls, pork pie, celery, chocolate penguin biscuits, date and walnut cake, apples, tea and orange squash. Then they went home.

In the evening Dinah Price watched TV for a while, and had a bath. When bedtime came, she kissed her mum and dad goodnight, climbed the stairs, went into her room – and found an upside-down boy in her bed.

The boy's feet were on the pillow. The rest of him

was under the bedclothes. Dinah guessed it was a boy from his socks. They were football socks and full of holes.

Dinah Price went up to the bed. A lump, which was the boy's head, was moving about under the bedclothes. Dinah gave it a tap. 'Excuse me!'

The lump stopped moving. A muffled voice said, 'Who is it?'

'It's me,' said Dinah.

'Oh,' said the voice. There was a pause. 'What do you want?'

Dinah tapped the lump again. She liked doing it. 'I want you to get out of the bed.'

There was another pause. The lump moved round in a circle. Finally, the bedclothes became untucked on one side, and a boy's head appeared. He had blue eyes and freckles. His hair was all over the place. His collar was turned up; his tie twisted to one side. He looked quite old, Dinah thought: about fourteen.

The boy blinked and stared at Dinah. 'Who are you?'

'I'm Dinah Price,' said Dinah. 'Who are you?'

'Let's see,' said the boy. 'It's on the tip of my tongue. *Simple Simon met a pieman going to* ... I'm Simple Simon!'

Dinah sat down on her stool. Simple Simon remained with his head sticking out from the bedclothes. His feet were on the pillow again. He was in a sort of 'L' shape.

'What were you doing in there?' said Dinah.

'Seeing what it was like,' said Simon. 'Of course it's pretty dark, you know. You need a torch really – or a candle.'

'That would set the bed on fire!'

'That's true,' said Simon. 'Then you would need a bucket of water.'

'Then you would need another bed!'

'That's true,' said Simon.

Dinah looked at Simple Simon's feet. He was drumming with them on the pillow. She looked round the room and under the bed. 'Where are your shoes?'

'I swopped them,' said Simon.

'What for?'

'For the socks.'

'What happened to your own socks?'

'I swopped them for a ride on another boy's bike.'

Now Simple Simon looked round the room. He said, 'This is a nice room. I wish I had a room like this. What's in that wardrobe?'

'Clothes,' said Dinah.

'You could live in a wardrobe, you know.' At this point Simple Simon pulled his head in and began to burrow up the bed. His once more muffled voice continued: 'I am going to go round the world one of these days. I think I might be a school teacher – or a cook.' Then his head popped out again, this time on the pillow.

By now, of course, the bed had become quite untidy. Dinah said, 'You are making a mess of my bed. I will get into trouble for that.'

'Oh!' Simon looked worried. 'Is this *your* bed?'

'Yes,' said Dinah.

'Well, what am I doing in it?'

'That's what I want to know.'

'Who will you get into trouble with?' said Simon. 'An ogre?'

'No – my mum and dad.'

Simple Simon scratched his head. 'I know a poem about an ogre. It goes:

> *Fe Fo Fe . . .*
> *Fe Fum Fo . . .*
> *Fe . . . er,*
> *Fe . . .*

Well, I *did* know it.' He whistled briefly and glanced up at the ceiling. 'I know a poem about *me*! It goes:

> *Simple Simon met a pieman*
> *Going to the fair.*
> *Said Simple Simon to the pieman,*
> *Give me one of those pies!'*

'*Let me taste your ware,*' said Dinah.

'What?'

'*Let me taste your ware.* That's what it should say. Besides, what you said doesn't rhyme.'

'It tastes better, though,' said Simon. 'Who wants *ware*?'

'I don't think it makes any difference,' said Dinah. 'You had no money, so he didn't sell you a pie anyway.'

'Who told you that?'

'I read it in a book.'

'You *read* it?' Simple Simon stared admiringly at Dinah. 'That's clever. Yes . . . I wish I could read. If I could read, I could be a man who sticks posters up.'

Once more Simon looked round the room. He put a finger in his mouth and made a popping noise with his cheek. 'This is a comfy bed. I wonder whose it is?'

'It's mine,' said Dinah. 'I already told you.'

'So you did . . . What did you say your name was?'

'Dinah!' said Dinah.

'Ah, yes.' Simon began to snuggle down the bed.

Dinah said, 'Don't get too comfy. It's going-home time.'

Simon looked puzzled.

'Home time,' said Dinah. 'Time to leave!'

'Leave?' Simon still looked puzzled. 'Where are you going?'

'Not me – you!'

'Me? Where am I going?'

'How should I know?' said Dinah. 'Where did you come from?'

'Don't ask me!' said Simon.

At this point Simple Simon began to empty his pockets. In front of him on the bed he made a pile of: sweet-papers, pencil stubs, marbles, a comic, a conker

on a shoe-lace, rubber bands, a balloon, two cotton reels, three sardine tin-openers and a few other things. Finally, he found what he was looking for: a paper bag with a pie in it. Simon removed the pie and examined it closely. He sniffed it too.

'That's a pie!' said Dinah.

'Yes: meat and potato. Do you want a bite?'

Dinah shook her head. 'No thank you.' Then she said, 'Did you get that pie from the pieman? I thought you didn't have any money.'

'I swopped him,' said Simon.

'What for?'

'Well, actually it was for two other pies. I think I made a mistake there.'

Simple Simon took a bite from his pie and gazed contentedly round the room. 'I wish I had a room like this. What's in that wardrobe?'

'Same as before,' said Dinah. 'Clothes.'

'You could live in a wardrobe, you know,' said Simon.

Now Dinah looked puzzled. She left her stool and stood at the window. It was getting dark. Low clouds were flying across the sky. A cat went sauntering down the garden. It disappeared among the rhododendron bushes. Dinah turned back into the room. 'Listen – this is what we will do. I will tell you a story, and then –'

'No, don't do that,' said Simon. 'I don't like stories. When anybody tells me a story, I always feel sorry for the ones who *don't* live happily ever after: older brothers, for instance. You see, what I've noticed is, it's always the youngest brother who finds the magic ring or whatever it is, and marries the princess. I am an older brother myself.'

'What about dragons and wicked step-mothers, though? Do you feel sorry for them?'

'I do. I think to myself: it's not their fault; they didn't write it.' Simon began to flick his ears with his fingers. 'You know, sometimes I think to myself, *I* am in a story.'

'Well, you are,' said Dinah. 'You're in *Simple Simon*.'

'That's true; though it would have been *Brainy Simon* or *Captain Dynamite Simon*, if I had written it.'

'Perhaps *I* am in a story!' said Dinah.

'You probably are.' Simon was pulling a thread of wool from the sleeve of his jumper. 'Sometimes I think to myself, everybody is.'

Now Dinah began to get impatient. She explained to Simon that really it was time he went home, wherever it was. She had to go to sleep. She would get into trouble if she didn't.

'Who will you get into trouble with?' said Simon. 'An ogre?'

'Never mind about that!' Dinah could see she would have to be strict. 'Come on – out!' She pulled the bedclothes back. 'All the others went home – even the wicked witch – even the wolf!'

Simple Simon sat on the bed. 'I know a poem about a wolf.'

'I don't want to hear it,' said Dinah. 'Now then, put these things back in your pockets.'

'But I'm still eating this pie.'

'Well, hurry up!' said Dinah.

Finally, when Simon had eaten his pie, and brushed the crumbs from his jumper, and filled his pockets again, Dinah directed him to the window.

'Is this the way out?' said Simon. 'I usually use the door.'

'You can go down the drainpipe. The Three Bears did; so did Sleeping Beauty.'

'If this was a story,' said Simon, 'and I was writing it, I'd write two endings. Then I could go down the drainpipe in one, and out the door in the other.'

'I never thought of that,' said Dinah.

Simple Simon sat on the window ledge. He breathed on the window and steamed it up. He began to draw a face. 'If we had plenty of time –'

'We don't have plenty of time.'

'But if we did,' said Simon, 'we could wait here for the tree to grow till it reached the window, and I could climb out. Or we could wait for the ground to rise or the house to sink, and I could walk out.'

Simple Simon took hold of the drainpipe. 'England was joined to France once, you know. You could just walk over. The world used to be flat then, a man told me.' He began to descend. 'Yes – then, somehow or other it got blown up, the man said . . . like a balloon.'

Dinah leant out of the window to watch Simple Simon as he went down. When he reached the bottom, he looked round and scratched his head. 'Which way do I go?'

Dinah pointed down the garden. 'That way!'

'I think I will be an explorer one of these days,' said Simon. He set off across the grass in his stockinged feet. He had his hands in his pockets and was whistling *The Teddy Bears' Picnic*.

Dinah watched him go, and – shortly after – saw him disappear among the rhododendron bushes. She breathed on the window and drew a cat in the steam. She shut the window, pulled the curtains across and got into bed. 'I will tell my friend about this tomorrow,' Dinah said to herself. She closed her eyes – and slept till morning.

7

A Kiss

I'll get you

The next day Dinah Price got up, got dressed and had her breakfast. She had toast and marmalade – there weren't any cornflakes – a cup of tea and an orange. She had a dip with her toast in her dad's boiled egg. She told her dad about Simple Simon. He said that was very interesting. Her mum said it was very interesting too. Now we know why the bed was such a mess, she said.

On her way to school Dinah remembered her dinner-money, which she had left on the kitchen table. She ran back to fetch it. In the playground she told her friend about Simple Simon. But her friend was being chased by a boy and didn't listen.

During the morning Dinah read her book to Mrs Hicks and did some writing. When the flowers got knocked over, she fetched the mop.

The school dinner was salad and sausage roll; chocolate sponge and custard. The chocolate sponge had hundreds and thousands on it.

After dinner Dinah played with her friend on the climbing-frame. The boy who had chased her friend came and chased her again. He got his friend to chase Dinah.

When she came home from school, Dinah went to the shop for her mum. She fetched a packet of tea and a box of cornflakes. She ate an apple and played with her baby brother in the garden. She wanted to play with her big brother in the park; but he was going with his friends and wouldn't take her.

After tea Dinah put her goldfish in a bucket and cleaned the tank out. When bedtime came, she kissed her mum and dad goodnight, kissed her big brother too, who was eating a bag of crisps and didn't notice, climbed the stairs, went into her room – and found *nobody* in her bed.

Dinah looked round the room and behind the door. She looked at the wardrobe but not in it. She listened to the faint sound from the television downstairs. She slipped her slippers off and got into bed.

'Hey!' said a voice. 'Have a care here – this bed is occupied!'

'Oh!' Dinah jumped back. She peered more closely at the bed. There *was* somebody in it. Tucked in, with the blankets up to his chin – in as far as he had one – and a little crown on his head, was the Frog Prince.

Dinah sat on the stool. She knew hardly anything about the Frog Prince. She had heard of him, and perhaps seen his picture somewhere, but that was about all.

The Frog Prince, meanwhile, had hopped onto the pillow. He was mopping the back of his neck – in as far as he had one – with a little hankie. 'That was a near thing. You could have flattened me there.'

'I'm very sorry,' said Dinah.

'Never mind; it happens all the time.' The frog tucked the hankie into a little rucksack, which he had beside him. He looked more closely at Dinah. 'Are you the owner of this bed, may I ask?'

'Yes,' said Dinah.

'Right – let us get down to business. Are you a princess?'

'No,' said Dinah.

'How do you know? You could be a princess and not know it.'

'My name is Dinah Price,' said Dinah.

'What is your father's name?'

'Mr Price.'

'I confess it is not hopeful.' The Frog Prince had removed a tiny notebook from his rucksack and was turning its pages. 'There again, maybe he is not your real father. Maybe you were stolen away from some palace or other when you were a baby, and are being brought up now as their own child by an honest wood-cutter and his wife.'

'My dad works at the window-frame factory,' said Dinah. 'He's a foreman.' Then she said, 'Could I really have been stolen away?'

'Certainly. It happens all the time.' The frog put the notebook beside him on the pillow. 'Anyway, the thing is . . .' He rubbed his eye as though he had something in it. 'The thing is . . . will you give me kiss?'

'A kiss?' said Dinah. 'What for?'

'To turn me into a prince, that's what for!' Again the frog consulted his notebook. 'But I can tell you are not familiar with the story. You see, I am not really a frog; I am a prince. What happened was, a wicked witch – for reasons I need not go into – turned me into a frog. Now the only way I'll –'

'Did she have a wart on her nose?' said Dinah.

'I don't remember.'

'Did you rattle a stick along her garden fence?'

'Not that I recall. Anyway, as I was saying; now the only way I'll be a prince again, is if a princess kisses me. So . . .' Once more the frog rubbed his eye. 'How about it?'

'I can't kiss you,' said Dinah. 'I hardly know you.'

'What is there to know?'

'Also, you are a frog!'

'Of course – that's the whole point!' Despite his natural politeness, the frog was showing signs of exasperation. 'I am a frog: you are a princess – or might be. You kiss me: I turn into a prince. We get married: my father gives us half his kingdom –'

'I can't get married. I'm not old enough.'

'I'll wait for you,' said the frog.

'No,' said Dinah.

'I'll give you this notebook' – the frog was rummaging in his rucksack – 'pencil, penknife, ordnance survey map, adjustable spanner –'

'No,' said Dinah.

The frog grew frantic. He tipped the rucksack's contents onto the pillow. 'I'll give you everything I've got! I'll even throw in the rucksack!'

'No,' said Dinah.

For a moment there was silence. A breeze rustled the leaves on the tree outside the window. A fly was buzzing about. Downstairs the phone began to ring.

The Frog Prince sighed, and his shoulders – in as far as he had any – drooped. 'I understand. I guess I would not kiss a frog either, if the truth were known.' He began to return things to his rucksack. 'There again, at least you have not tried to cheat me, which some of them do.'

'Do they?' said Dinah. She felt sorry for the frog and would have cheered him up, if she could.

'Certainly. Some princesses are not to be trusted, in my experience. They will cause you to do all manner of things, promise you this and that – and then set the dog on you.'

The frog completed his packing, except for the notebook and pencil, which he kept beside him. 'I had an example only the other day. There was this princess playing with a golden ball – by the way, you wouldn't have anything to eat, would you?'

'No,' said Dinah. Then she thought of the fly, which

was still buzzing about. 'There's a fly, though. Frogs eat flies, Mrs Hicks says.'

'This frog doesn't,' said the frog. 'Thanks all the same. Anyway, as I was saying; there was this princess playing with a golden ball, which was her favourite plaything, right next to a pond. Well, of course, the ball went into the pond and sank. "Alas!" the princess cried. "If I could only get my ball again." Well, I was hopping by at the time, so I said I would get it for her, if she gave me a kiss, which was fair enough, and she thought for a minute and said she would.'

'And did she?' said Dinah.

'I am coming to that. So then I dived into the pond

and with much difficulty, I can tell you, hunted round
in the mud at the bottom – that was a messy business –
got the golden ball in my mouth, which nearly choked
me, and brought it back to her.'

'I bet she was pleased,' said Dinah.

'She was. She was so pleased, she picked up that ball
and – with never a thought for me – ran off home as
fast as she could. "Stay, princess!" I shouted.
"Remember your promise!" But she just kept going.
Of course, I hopped after her, which took an age; that
pond was at the far end of the palace gardens. Then I
had to climb a huge flight of stairs even to reach the
front door. Actually, I had to climb it twice. A gardener

spotted me the first time and carried me down again. Anyway, I knocked on the door, saying – I'm supposed to speak in verse, you know – saying:

> *Open the door, my princess dear.*
> *Open the door to your true love here.*
> *Remember the promise that you made*
> *By the fountain cool in the greenwood shade.'*

'You said it was a pond,' said Dinah.

'Well, there were fountains too,' said the frog. 'Besides, it's more poetic. So anyway, I said all that, and she came out with her mother, the queen, denied the whole thing and – like I said – set the dog on me.'

'Oh dear!' said Dinah.

'Yes. Luckily dogs are not partial to frogs, or I would not be here to tell the tale.' The frog removed his little crown and scratched his head. 'There again, I could have jumped to safety, I suppose. We frogs can jump, if nothing else. Watch this!' He placed his crown on the pillow and took a flying leap. It carried him almost to the foot of the bed.'

'That's clever!' said Dinah.

The frog turned and repeated his jump back onto the pillow. 'Now then' – he was puffing slightly – 'while I remember – let me make a note of your name.' He reached for his notebook and pencil. 'I like to keep a list of those I meet.'

Dinah Price leant forward. She peered at the pages of the notebook and the tiny writing which covered them. 'You must have met lots of people.'

'That's true; lots and lots – princesses mostly, of course. How do you spell "Dinah"?'

Dinah told him.

'Yes,' said the frog, 'lots and lots; beautiful and not so beautiful, tall and short, old and young – babies even!'

'Your writing's good,' said Dinah. 'It's joined up.' Then she said, 'Babies?'

'Babies,' said the frog. 'Oh yes, I was with a baby princess only this morning. She was in her high-chair in the royal kitchen. Well, there is no age-limit from my point of view, you see. So I thought to myself, this is it! You will get a kiss here. She is a baby and will not know any better.'

'What happened?' said Dinah.

'She was eating a rice pudding and hit me with the spoon. Not maliciously, you understand. Babies don't appreciate their own strength.'

At this point the frog reached for his rucksack. He put his notebook and pencil in one of the pockets. He slipped his little arms through the straps and heaved it on.

'Oh,' said Dinah. 'Are you going home now?'

'Going: yes,' said the frog. 'Home: no.' He hopped to the side of the bed, lay on his stomach and looked over the edge. 'Which is the best way?'

Dinah thought for a minute. She said, 'I could tie my skipping ropes together ... and the cord from my dressing-gown and – yes! – and lower you in a basket out of the window.'

'What sort of basket?'

'It had my Easter egg in it.' Dinah fetched the basket and put it on the bed.

The Frog Prince hopped round it, in and out of it, and up and down in it. He hopped up and down in it to test its strength. 'This'll do,' he said.

After that the frog allowed himself to be carried in the basket to the window-sill. He looked out into the garden. So did Dinah.

'Will you be all right?'

'Perfectly,' said the frog. 'I have a head for heights. Why, only last week I came upon a princess – I haven't told you this one, have I? No – a princess who, for reasons I need not go into, was sleeping on a pile of twenty mattresses and twenty feather beds.'

'Goodness!' said Dinah.

'Yes. Well, I climbed up and up and up, and never turned a hair. Surely I will get a kiss for this, I thought.' The frog paused and studied the knots which Dinah was tying. 'The trouble was, it took so long, the princess was up and out the other side before I got there.'

'That was bad luck,' said Dinah.

'Yes.' The frog hopped out of the basket and into it again. 'Well, it has been nice meeting you.' He held out his little hand, which Dinah with her finger and thumb was just able to shake.

'It has been nice meeting *you*,' said Dinah.

'Right then,' said the frog. 'Lower away!'

Dinah began to lower the basket down into the garden. Suddenly she came to a decision and hauled it up again.

'What's happening?' said the frog, as his head appeared once more above the window-sill.

Dinah Price did not reply, but leant forward and – blushing slightly – kissed the frog on his forehead, in as far as he had one. 'There!' she said.

The frog remained a frog. This was probably just as well, considering he was still dangling in the basket. However, at least now he was a cheerful frog.

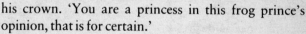

'Thank you, Dinah Price; I appreciate that.' He raised his crown. 'You are a princess in this frog prince's opinion, that is for certain.'

After that the basket reached the ground, and the frog hopped out. Then – turning once to wave goodbye – he set off across the grass, his rucksack on his back, to continue the search.

Dinah Price watched him go, or tried to. A green frog on green grass is not easy to see. And the rucksack was green too.

When the frog was out of sight, Dinah untied her skipping ropes and the cord from her dressing-gown.

She shut the window and pulled the curtains across. She got into bed, closed her eyes – and slept till morning.

8

Little Girl Sandwich

The next day Dinah Price got up, got dressed and had her breakfast. She had cornflakes with the top of the milk on them, a piece of her dad's toast and marmalade, a cup of tea and an orange. She told her dad about the Frog Prince. He said that was very interesting. Her mum said *she* would not kiss a frog, if you paid her.

On her way to school Dinah told her friend about the Frog Prince. Her friend told her about her wobbly tooth coming out. She showed Dinah the tooth – and the gap. She showed her the 10p too, which she had found under her pillow when she woke up.

At school Dinah drew a picture of the Frog Prince in her News Book. Her teacher, Mrs Hicks, said it was very nice dear.

The school dinner was Cumberland pie, peas and gravy; sponge cake and raspberry jelly.

In the afternoon Mrs Hicks's class put on their shorts and plimsolls, and had races on the school field. They had sack races, egg-and-spoon races, and three-legged races. Dinah liked the sack race best. She liked jumping up and down – I'm a frog, she thought – and the funny smell of the sack. She liked winning too, which is what she did.

After school Dinah's friend came to play and have tea at Dinah's house. They made a den in the garden with the box the new washing-machine had come in. They put Dinah's baby brother in it and played 'Peepo' with him. Then they had tea, and Dinah's friend went home.

When bedtime came, Dinah Price kissed her mum and dad goodnight. They were in the front garden making a rockery. Then Dinah kissed the dog too, although her dad said she shouldn't, climbed the stairs, went into her room – and found a giant in her bed.

Actually, this giant was quite a small giant. He was about as big as two-and-a-half men. He sat up in the bed with his feet sticking out. The bedclothes covered only a part of him. His arms reached to the floor; his head was up near the light-shade. Beside him on the bedside rug there was an enormous trilby hat, an enormous pair of boots, and a giant picnic basket.

84

Dinah Price looked at the giant and did not like what she saw. What she especially did not like was the monstrous dinner-plate on his lap, the huge knife and fork in his hands, and the sheet – her sheet – now tucked in the front of his shirt like a bib.

Dinah might well have gone onto the landing again, or downstairs even, but the door no longer opened. The giant – absentmindedly, it seemed – had wedged his foot against it.

Dinah Price knew a lot about giants. There was the giant in *Jack the Giant-Killer*, which Mrs Hicks had read to them. There was the one in *Jack and the Beanstalk*. Dinah had seen him in a pantomime last Christmas with her Auntie Annie and her Uncle Jim. There were others too, she could recall, which various princes or brave youngest sons had dealt with. Dinah comforted herself with the thought that giants, for all their size, mostly came off second-best.

The giant looked at Dinah Price. When he spoke, his voice was quiet and matter-of-fact. He said:

> '*Fe Fi Fo Fum*
> *I smell the blood of an Englishman –*'

'I'm not a man,' said Dinah.

The giant fumbled in his jacket pocket, took out a huge pair of spectacles and put them on. 'Woman,' he said. 'Girl!

> *Be he – she alive or be she dead*
> *I'll grind her bones to make my bread!*

There – what do you think of that?'

'It doesn't rhyme,' said Dinah. '"Girl" doesn't rhyme with "Fum".'

The giant looked thoughtful. 'You're right. Come to think of it, "man" doesn't either. Fancy that; all these years and I never noticed that before.'

'Also' – Dinah was gaining confidence from the giant's mild manner and quiet voice – 'also, you can't make bread out of bones; it wouldn't stick together. Or if it did, it would taste awful.'

'Right again,' said the giant. 'Although I would suggest that what we have here is more a figure of speech. You see, I don't intend to grind your bones exactly; I'm just going to eat you up.'

At this point the giant opened his giant picnic basket and took out a giant cruet-stand, containing salt cellar, pepper pot and mustard jar.

Dinah backed up into a corner of the room. She said, 'You can't eat me – I'm only a little girl!'

'Little girls taste the best,' said the giant. 'Didn't you know that?'

'You can't eat me,' said Dinah. 'It's not fair!'

'On the contrary, it's my duty as a giant. *Fish gotta swim, birds gotta fly* – and I have to eat people.' The giant took out a plastic box from his picnic basket. It contained huge slices of bread-and-butter. He put two of them on his plate. 'Come along now, no more arguments. If you were a youngest son, it might be different. Or,' he lowered his voice to an almost nervous whisper, 'or if your name was J.A.C.K.'

Dinah thought for a minute. 'That spells "Jack"!'

'Sh!' The giant put a finger to his lips. 'I prefer never to hear that name.' Then he said, 'Come along now, let us not delay. Climb up here and lie down on this bread-and-butter.'

Dinah felt hot tears begin to gather in her eyes. 'You

can't eat me!' She tried to think of a good reason. When she couldn't, she made one up. 'You can't eat me – my . . . my poor old mother will be all alone.'

'No, she won't,' said the giant, calmly. 'She is not old, I'm sure of that.' He glanced out of the window. 'Besides, whose are all those nappies on the line? You have got a baby sister, I'll be bound.'

'Brother,' said Dinah, before she could stop herself.

'Just as I thought – telling fibs!' The giant wagged a finger at Dinah. It was like a policeman's truncheon. 'That is a terrible thing, telling fibs at your age. You should be ashamed of yourself.' He began adjusting his bib. 'However, just you come and lie down in this sandwich, which I have ready for you, and we will say no more about it.'

'No,' said Dinah. Then she said, 'Sandwich?'

'Sandwich,' said the giant. 'I have not had a little girl sandwich in weeks. It's been that long, I ought to make a wish.'

Dinah felt the tears now on her cheeks. 'Don't put me into a sandwich. I will give you this woolly duck and these skipping ropes.'

'No,' said the giant.

'I will give you all my books and dolls, my set of felt pens, my goldfish – no, not them – my pencil-sharpener and my Easter egg basket. I will give you everything I've got!'

'No,' said the giant.

Dinah grew frantic. 'Well, I will tell you a story then. That's it: I will tell you a story. After that you will get out of the bed and I will get into it. Then you will go home to your *own* bed, and I will go to sleep.'

At this point the giant tried to interrupt, but Dinah

just kept going. 'Once upon a time there was a poor old woman who lived in a little cottage on the edge of a wood. It was a pretty cottage, this cottage was. It had a red roof, yellow curtains and roses round the door. Well, this old woman, she had a son and his name was Ja – George.'

'Are you sure of that?' said the giant.

'Yes – George. Well, one day this old woman sent George to the market to sell the cow because they were so poor and needed the money, only he swopped the cow for some coloured beans, you see, and this made the old woman so angry she threw those beans out of the window and beat George with her broomstick, only then, when George got up the next morning, there was a great big beanstalk growing in the garden and –'

'Pardon me,' said the giant, 'but I have heard this story before. It is not one of my favourites.'

'I'll change it,' said Dinah.

'No thank you. I would prefer to have my supper.' The giant put out his hand to pick Dinah up.

'Help!' shouted Dinah.

'Come along now,' said the giant. 'This bread-and-butter will be getting dry.'

'Help!' shouted Dinah.

'What is more, you could wake your baby sister up with all that noise.'

'Brother,' shouted Dinah. 'Help!'

'Sh!' said the giant. 'Show some consideration.'

'Help, help, help!'

At that moment, when all seemed lost, there came a loud wailing noise from across the landing. It was Dinah's baby brother – little Maurice – howling his head off.

Dinah Price looked at the giant, and the giant looked at Dinah Price. Both had guilty expressions on their faces.

'There,' said the giant. 'Now look what you've done.'

'Now look what *you've* done,' said Dinah. 'You started it.'

'Waaaa!' cried the baby.

'You started it,' said Dinah.

'You were going to eat me.'

'I still am,' said the giant.

'Help!'

'All right, all right, let's not have that again. I won't eat you . . .'
The giant lowered his voice, '. . . for a while.'

'Waaaa!' cried the baby.

The giant continued to look uneasy. 'Poor little thing! He sounds like he's about to explode in there. Why doesn't somebody come? Where's your mum and dad?'

'In the front garden,' said Dinah; 'making a rockery.'

'It's a disgrace – leaving a little baby like that.'

'Waaaa!' cried the baby.

'I could go,' said Dinah. 'I could stop him crying.'

'No – you'd go, and that would be the last I'd see of you. I've had sandwiches run off from me before.'

'Well, *you* go then!'

'No, that's no use. I never know what to say to babies.'

'Waaaa!' cried the baby.

The giant sighed and fingered his bib. 'That noise is putting me off. I am losing my appetite.'

'I don't see why you should eat me, anyway,' said Dinah. She had thought of another reason. 'How would you like it?'

'What do you mean?'

'How would you like it, if an even bigger giant came into *your* room and wanted to put *you* in a sandwich?'

The giant looked thoughtful. 'You have a point there. Come to think of it, how would *he* like it if an even bigger giant came into his room and wanted to put *him* in a sandwich?'

'Yes,' said Dinah. 'And how would *HE* like it?'

'This thing could go on for ever,' said the giant. He toyed with his bread-and-butter. 'Fancy that: me in a sandwich! All these years and I never thought of that before.'

And the baby cried, 'Waaaa!'

The giant winced. He looked at Dinah; she looked at him. Then, without a word, he moved his foot which was blocking the door, and Dinah stepped out on to the landing and into her baby brother's room.

Her baby brother was very red in the face. He had become tangled up in his cot blanket and was thrashing around. Dinah tidied the cot and stroked the baby's damp hair. She kissed him on his forehead. She gave him a finger to hold. The baby stopped crying almost at once. He stared up at Dinah with great interest. He squeezed her finger in his powerful grip and put it in his mouth.

When the baby was peaceful again and dozing off, Dinah returned to the landing. She listened at her bedroom door and heard the giant's heavy breathing. She peeped in. The giant was still in the bed. He was eating his bread-and-butter, and reading one of Dinah's books. It looked more like a postage stamp in his enormous hand.

Dinah thought for a minute, then crept downstairs. Her big brother was in the playroom with his friend watching T.V. There was a football match on. Dinah went into the front room and looked out of the window. It was getting dark, but her mum and dad were still at work. The next-door neighbour was leaning on the fence talking to them. Then Dinah's dad stood up and wiped his forehead on his rolled-up sleeve, and spotted Dinah.

'Hey – what's this?' He pointed at her with his trowel. 'Come on, young lady – back to bed!'

'But I've got a giant in there!' said Dinah, shouting through the glass.

'Tell him to move over!' said her dad.

And her mum said, 'Come on – off you go!'

Dinah didn't argue. From the expression on her mum's face – and her dad's – she knew it was no use; also her feet were getting cold. She left the room.

Before returning upstairs, Dinah took a piece of cheese and tomato flan from the pantry, and a small apple pie from a box in the kitchen. Back on the landing, she peeped once more into her room. But this time it was empty. She went inside – nothing! The giant and his giant boots and trilby hat were gone. So was the picnic basket.

Dinah stepped over to the window. It had been opened as wide as it would go. The evening breeze was lifting the curtains . . . and a giant face was peering in.

'I wasn't sure you were coming back,' said the giant. He had his hat on and his glasses off. 'I was thinking you were thinking I might still eat you.'

'Well . . .' said Dinah.

'I wouldn't do that,' the giant laughed. 'Besides, I

have eaten all the bread-and-butter. I couldn't make a sandwich, if I wanted to.'

'Well,' said Dinah, 'I have brought you a piece of cheese and tomato flan.'

The giant took the flan and examined it closely. 'I suppose I might have to get used to things like this. Cheese and tomato, you say?' He popped it into his mouth. 'Hmmm . . . not bad!'

'And an apple pie,' said Dinah.

The giant ate that too. For him it was like eating a Smartie.

Dinah said, 'I've just thought of something: how did you get out?'

The giant placed the foil cup from his apple pie on the window-sill. 'The same way I got in,' he said: 'with difficulty.'

After that he raised his trilby hat, said goodbye to Dinah Price and strode off across the garden in the direction of the allotments.

Dinah watched him go. His silhouette became smaller and darker as he went away. A blue and purple haze had gathered along the edge of the sky. A darker smudge of smoke rose from a factory chimney. Higher in the sky, the white trail of an aeroplane was stretching out in one direction, dissolving in the other.

Dinah glanced back into the room. The bed was a mess. Then she heard footsteps on the landing, and her mum came in.

'What's all this, Dinah?' said her mum. 'This bed's a mess!'

'The giant did it,' said Dinah.

'And the window's wide open!'

'The giant left it open.'

Dinah's mum spotted the foil cup on the window-sill. 'I suppose the giant ate this too.'

'Yes, he did,' said Dinah. 'And if you don't believe me – there he is!' She pointed out of the window.

'Where?'

'There!'

Dinah's mum stared out at the darkening horizon. Dinah stared too. Was it there? Was it? A distant giant shape moving away? Somehow, Dinah wasn't sure herself.

Dinah's mum shut the window and pulled the curtains across. 'Come on, young lady – back to bed!'

Dinah did not reply. She was uncertain what to say. She got into the bed. Her mum tidied it up around her, tucked her in and gave her a kiss.

'There *was* a giant,' said Dinah.

'Yes,' said her mum. She stroked Dinah's hair.

'There was a wolf too – and three bears, a frog prince, Simple Simon, Puss in Boots and Sleeping Beauty.'

'Yes,' said her mum.

'And a wicked witch!'

'Yes. Now – go to sleep.'

Dinah's mum crossed the room. She switched off the light and shut the door behind her. Dinah listened to the footsteps fading on the stairs. 'I will tell my friend about this tomorrow,' she said to herself.

After that she closed her eyes, turned over on her side – and slept till morning.